淘氣一族

Terry Dinning 著

Angela Kincaid 繪

陳培真 譯

三民書局

Read with Me Stories   ISBN 1 85854 749 0

Written by Terry Dinning and illustrated by Angela Kincaid

(Two stories: "Freddy Fox" and "Gilda the Witch")

First published in 1998

Under the title Read with Me Stories

by Brimax Books Limited

4/5 Studlands Park Ind. Estate,

Newmarket, Suffolk, CB8 7AU

"ⓒ 1998 Brimax Books Limited

All rights reserved"

My First Storybook   ISBN 1 85854 517 X

Illustrated by Angela Kincaid

(One story: "The Naughty Kitten")

First published in 1996

Under the title Read by Yourself

By Brimax Books Limited

4/5 Studlands Park Ind. Estate,

Newmarket, Suffolk, CB8 7AU

"ⓒ 1998 Brimax Books Limited

All rights reserved"

淘氣小貓咪
The Naughty Kitten

Ching and Chang are two
Siamese kittens.
They love **exploring**
the garden.
Everything has to be
sniffed and anything that **moves** has to be
chased. The trouble is that Chang is always
getting into **mischief**.

Siamese [ˌsaɪəˈmiz]
形 暹羅的

kitten [ˈkɪtn̩]
名 小貓

explore [ɪkˈsplor]
動 探險

sniff [snɪf]
動 嗅

move [muv]
動 移動

chase [tʃes]
動 追趕

mischief [ˈmɪstʃɪf]
名 惡作劇

小青和小昌是兩隻暹羅貓。
他們倆喜歡在花園裡探險——每樣東西
都要嗅一嗅；一有風吹草動,都要追一追。
麻煩的是,小昌總是會惡作劇一番。

Hardly a day goes by when he does not do something **naughty**. But because they look so much alike, Chang **makes sure** it is Ching who gets the **blame**.
One afternoon, after taking a **nap**, Chang **leaps** out of their basket.

naughty [`nɔtɪ]
形 淘氣的

make sure
確定

blame [blem]
名 責備

nap [næp]
名 小睡

leap [lip]
動 跳

幾乎沒有一天小昌是不鬧事的。但是因為他們倆長得太像了，小昌總是讓小青成為挨罵的那一個。
一天下午，午睡過後，小昌從他們倆的籃子裡跳了出來。

"Come on Ching,"
he says **excitedly**.
"Let's go and have
some fun."
"I'm not going out
anymore," says Ching. "I had to go without my
cream at **lunchtime** because of you."
"Please yourself," says Chang, and he
scampers off.

excitedly [ɪk`saɪtɪdlɪ]
副 興奮地

cream [krim]
名 奶油

lunchtime
[`lʌntʃˌtaɪm]
名 午餐時間

「來吧！小青。」他興奮地說。「我們去找
點兒樂子吧！」
「我不會再出去了啦！」小青說。「上回就
是因為你，害我午餐沒吃奶油就走了。」
「隨便你囉！」小昌說著，然後一溜煙地
跑掉了。

Ching **curls up** and tries to get back to sleep, but he cannot. So he **sets off** to find his brother.
To his surprise Chang is sitting quietly beside the garden pond washing his face. For once he is **behaving** himself.

小青蜷起身體，想要睡個回籠覺，可是睡不著，便起來去找他弟弟。
出乎他的意料之外，小昌正靜靜地坐在花園的水池旁洗臉。這是他第一次這麼乖呢！

Ching **hurries** to join him.
As he draws nearer,
he sees something
that makes his fur
stand on end. A
glance in the pond

and Ching's **fears** are **confirmed**. Oscar's ball
is in the pond!
Oscar is a big dog. He lives in the same
house as the kittens, but he does not like
them one little bit. The ball in the pond is the
thing Oscar loves most in the world.

小青趕忙過去找他。當小青靠近一點兒
的時候，他看見了讓他毛骨悚然的事情。
小青瞄了一眼池塘，真的太可怕了。奧斯
卡的球在池子裡面哪！
奧斯卡是一隻大狗。他和小貓咪們住在
同個屋子裡，可是他一點兒也不喜歡他
們。水池裡的球正是奧斯卡最最珍愛的
東西。

"Ch.. Ch.. Chang,"
Ching **stammers**.
"What have you
done?"
Chang stops
washing and glances **innocently** at his
shaking brother. "What is the matter? I have
not done anything," he **replies**.
Ching looks again at the pond.

stammer [ˋstæmɚ]
動 口吃

innocently [ˋɪnəsn̩tlɪ]
副 無辜地

shake [ʃek]
動 發抖

reply [rɪˋplaɪ]
動 回答

「小……小……小昌，」小青結結巴巴了起
來。「你做了什麼好事啊？」
小昌停止洗臉，無辜地瞄了一眼他那發
抖的哥哥。「怎麼啦？我什麼都沒做哦！」
他回答說。
小青又看了看水池。

"But you have," Ching **insists**. "Oscar's ball is in the pond," he says in **horror**.

"What ball?" says **crafty** Chang. "I have not seen any ball," he **grins**.

Then he **shoots** off and **hides** in the **bushes**.

insist [ɪn`sɪst]
動 堅持

horror [`hɔrɚ]
名 恐懼

crafty [`kræftɪ]
形 狡猾的

grin [grɪn]
動 咧嘴笑

shoot [ʃut]
動 疾走

hide [haɪd]
動 躲藏

bush [buʃ]
名 矮樹叢

「你一定有。」小青堅持。「奧斯卡的球在池子裡面哪！」他非常害怕地說。
「什麼球啊？」狡猾的小昌說。「我沒看到什麼球啊！」他嘻皮笑臉地說。
然後他就一溜煙地跑開，躲到矮樹叢中去了。

Poor Ching is so worried about getting the blame that he feels like running away and never coming back.

He **gazes** in **despair** at the pond, he does not know what to do. Then suddenly he has an idea. Ching knows that his brother is a very good **swimmer** and he **decides** to play a **trick** on him.

gaze [gez]
動 盯著看

despair [dɪˋspɛr]
名 絕望

swimmer [ˋswɪmɚ]
名 游泳者

decide [dɪˋsaɪd]
動 決定

trick [trɪk]
名 惡作劇

可憐的小青十分擔心會挨罵，真想跑掉，絕不要再回來。
他絕望地盯著池子，不知道怎麼辦才好。突然，他靈機一動。小青知道他弟弟是個游泳好手，決定要捉弄他一次。

"Chang! Chang! Come quickly!" he **bellows**. "There is something horrible in our pond!"

Ching knows that his brother is not only naughty but very **nosy** as well. Almost at once Chang **leaves** his hiding place and **bounds** across the grass to look.

bellow [ˈbɛlo]
動 喊叫

nosy [ˈnozɪ]
形 好管閒事的

leave [liv]
動 離開

bound [baund]
動 蹦跳

「小昌！小昌！快過來！」他大聲喊叫。「我們的池子裡有恐怖的東西啊！」
小青很清楚他弟弟不僅調皮，而且也很愛管閒事。小昌幾乎馬上就離開他躲藏的地方，跳過草地來瞧瞧。

"Where?" he shouts and stares excitedly into the water.

"Right near the **edge**," says Ching pretending to be afraid.

Chang walks over to the edge of the pond and **stoops** for a closer look. Ching **lifts** his **paw** and gives him a **shove**. SPLASH! Chang falls into the water.

A very wet and a very angry Chang **climbs** out of the pond.

edge [ɛdʒ]
名 邊緣

stoop [stup]
動 彎腰

lift [lɪft]
動 舉起

paw [pɔ]
名 爪，腳掌

shove [ʃʌv]
名 猛推

climb [klaɪm]
動 爬

「哪兒呀？」他大叫，興奮地盯著池子裡看。

「就在靠近池邊的地方哪！」小青假裝很害怕地說。

小昌走過去池邊，彎下身來要瞧個仔細。這時小青舉起腳掌，推了小昌一把。噗通一聲！小昌跌進水池。

全身溼答答的小昌非常氣憤地從池子裡爬了出來。

The sight of his soaking wet brother makes Ching **roar** with **laughter**. A water lily is **stuck** to his head and **weeds** are **hanging** around his neck and **tripping** him up as he walks.

"Oh dear!" laughs Ching, who by now is lying on the grass with his feet in the air.

Chang is very angry.

roar [ror]
動 大叫

laughter [ˋlæftɚ]
名 笑，笑聲

stick [stɪk]
動 插

weed [wid]
名 雜草

hang [hæŋ]
動 垂掛

trip [trɪp]
動 使（人）絆倒

小青看到弟弟一副落湯雞的模樣，捧腹大笑了起來。一朵睡蓮插在小昌的頭上，脖子上垂繞著的水草讓他走路時絆倒。
「天啊！」小青這時笑得四腳朝天，躺在草地上。
小昌氣得不得了。

"hat did you do that for?" he shouts.
"Well, Oscar's ball is in the water," says Ching.
"I know that. It fell in while I was playing with it," says Chang **angrily**.
"I know," Ching **chuckles**, "but as the ball is in the water and you are the kitten who is wet, this time you will get the blame."

angrily [ˈæŋgrəlɪ]
副 生氣地

chuckle [ˈtʃʌkl̩]
動 咯咯地笑

「你為什麼要這樣做啊？」他吼了起來。
「嗯！奧斯卡的球在水裡面。」小青說。
「我知道啊！我玩到一半它就掉進去了！」小昌很生氣地說。
「我知道，」小青咯咯地笑，「現在球在水裡面，而你又全身溼答答的，這回要挨罵的人是你了。」

Chang **realizes**
how **clever** his
brother has been.
"So there is not
anything horrible
in the pond **after all**?"
he asks.
"Not now," says Ching. "It just **crawled** out!"
and taking to his **heels** he **disappears** behind
the garden **shed**.

realize [ˋrɪəˌlaɪz]
勔 了解

clever [ˋklɛvɚ]
形 聰明的

after all
終於，到底

crawl [krɔl]
勔 爬行

heel [hil]
名 腳跟

disappear [ˌdɪsəˋpɪr]
勔 消失

shed [ʃɛd]
名 小屋

小昌這才知道哥哥是多聰明！
「所以池子裡根本沒有什麼恐怖的東西
囉？」他問。
「現在沒了，它剛剛爬走了！」小青邊說，
邊拔腿就跑，消失在花園的小屋子後面。

Say these words again.

angry

afraid

surprise

something

replies

nosey

mischief

scampers

naughty

horror

suddenly

bounds

What did you see?

kittens

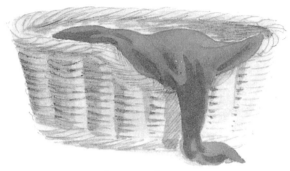

basket

ball

water lily

pond

中英對照，既可學英語又可了解偉人小故事哦！

超級科學家系列
SUPER SCIENTISTS

當彗星掠過哈雷眼前，
當蘋果落在牛頓頭頂，
當電燈泡在愛迪生手中亮起……
一個個求知的心靈與真理所碰撞出的火花，
就是《超級科學家系列》！

光的顏色
牛頓的故事

爆炸性的發現
諾貝爾的故事

命運的彗星
哈雷的故事

電燈的發明
愛迪生的故事

望遠天際
伽利略的故事

蠶寶寶的祕密
巴斯德的故事

宇宙教授
愛因斯坦的故事

神祕元素
居禮夫人的故事

神祕元素：居禮夫人的故事
電燈的發明：愛迪生的故事
望遠天際：伽利略的故事
光的顏色：牛頓的故事
爆炸性的發現：諾貝爾的故事
蠶寶寶的祕密：巴斯德的故事
宇宙教授：愛因斯坦的故事
命運的彗星：哈雷的故事

網際網路位址　http : // www. sanmin. com. tw

ⓒ 淘氣小貓咪

著作人　Terry Dinning
繪圖者　Angela Kincaid
譯　者　陳培真
發行人　劉振強
著作財　三民書局股份有限公司
產權人
　　　　臺北市復興北路三八六號
發行所　三民書局股份有限公司
　　　　地址／臺北市復興北路三八六號
　　　　電話／二五○○六六○○
　　　　郵撥／○○○九九九八——五號
印刷所　三民書局股份有限公司
門市部　復北店／臺北市復興北路三八六號
　　　　重南店／臺北市重慶南路一段六十一號
初　版　中華民國八十八年十一月
編　號　S85539
定　價　新臺幣壹佰陸拾元整
行政院新聞局登記證局版臺業字第○二○○號

ISBN　957-14-3086-2（精裝）

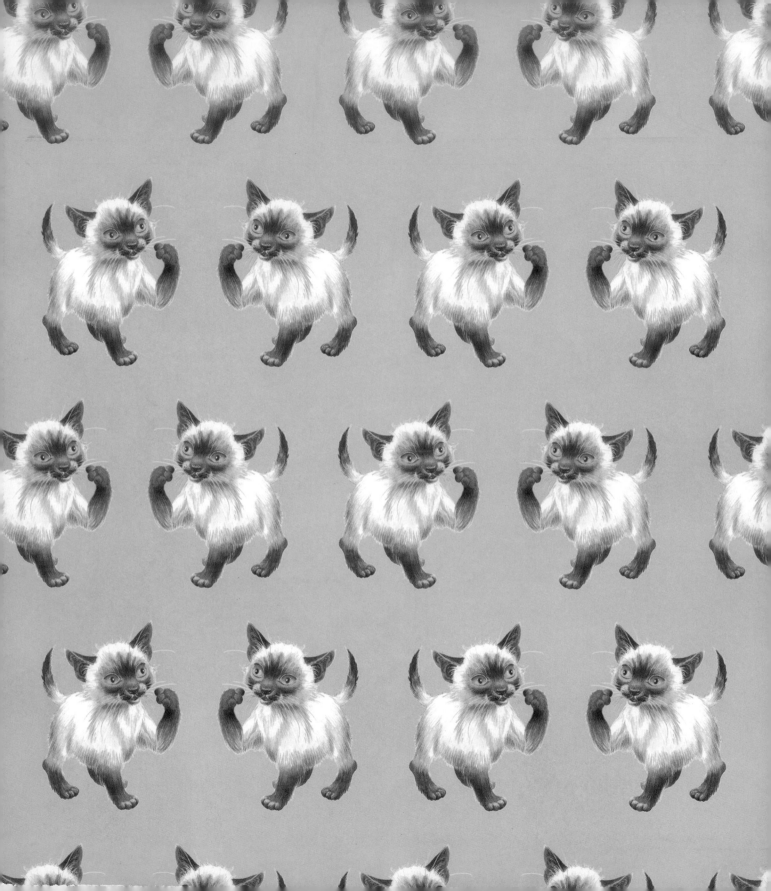